Newton and Me

$$a = F_{net}/m$$

By Lynne Mayer   Illustrated by Sherry Rogers

Saturday morning I was asleep in my bed,
when Newton, my dog, dropped his ball on my head.

I pulled on my blue jeans, t-shirt, and shoes and ate a quick breakfast while Dad read the news.

Then Newton and I ran out the back door.
We had the whole day to play and explore.

I rolled Newton's ball to him along the ground.
As we played with the ball, here's what we found . . .

The ball won't roll far in the rough, grassy yard.

It rolls much farther on a surface that's smooth and hard.

But, it won't roll at all if I don't give it a push.

When I pushed too hard, it rolled as far as the bush.

I decided to throw the ball up in the sky.
I threw the ball hard. It went really high.

No matter how hard I would throw the ball up,
it would always come down to me and my pup.

This gave me an idea I wanted to test.
I took out the red truck that I like the best.

I put down the truck on ground that was flat.
Until I would push, my truck stayed where it sat.

Going downhill my truck really speeds.
It went off the sidewalk and up into the weeds.

When I pushed my toy truck, it went really far.
But even my big push won't move my dad's car.

I heard my mom calling for Newton and me.
She wanted some rocks from a pile by the tree.

We pulled my red wagon to the tree at a run.
Newton and I knew this job would be fun.

filled up my wagon with piles of stone,
but with all of the rocks, I couldn't pull it alone.

When it was empty, it was easy to pull.
I just couldn't move it when it was full.

Newton and I got some help from my dad.
He pushed while I pulled. We made my mom glad.

Then Newton and I decided to go for a ride.
I hopped on my bike with my dog by my side.

The wind was blowing quite hard that day.
The wind at my back pushed me on my way.

But when I turned around to go home at last,
the wind pushed against my chest
and I couldn't go as fast.

Pedaling uphill was really hard too.
Getting to the top took all I could do.

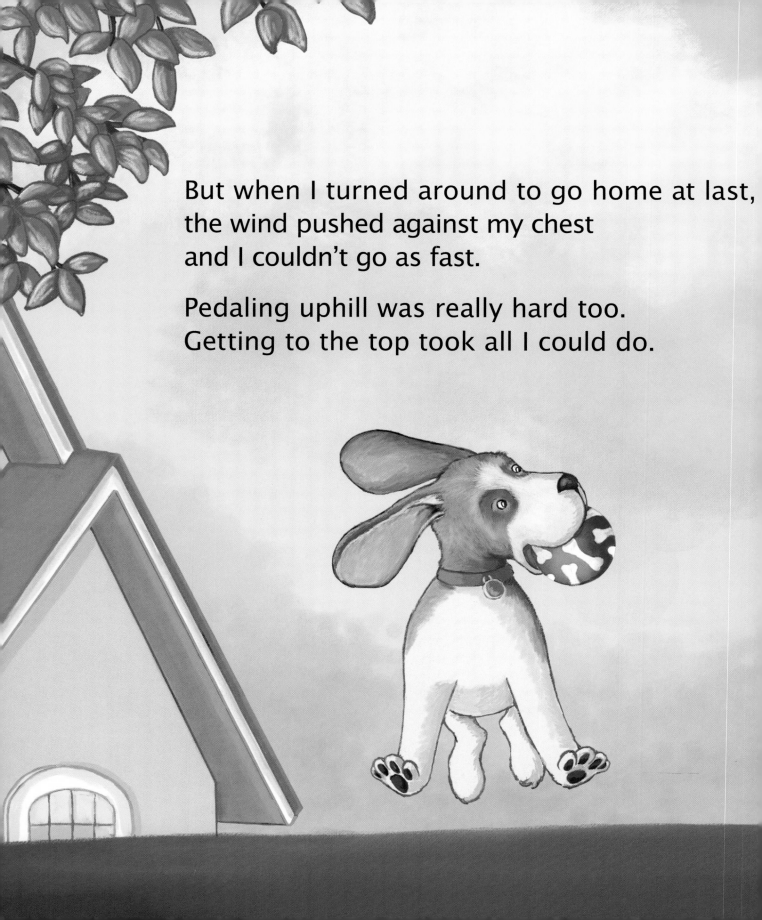

But going downhill, I needed to slow down.
I did that by dragging my feet on the ground.

When we got home, we played tug-of-war.
I pulled, Newton pulled, and then I pulled some more.

When he pulled as hard as I did, we didn't move at all.
But when he pulled harder, I'd step forward or fall.

realized at the end of the day
that I learned some new things along the way . . .

Playing with Newton gave me the notion
that pushing and pulling are forces of motion.

For Creative Minds

Force and Motion

A pull is a force that moves something toward you. *What are some things in the book that the boy pulls? What are some things that you might pull?*

A push is a force that moves something away from you. *What are some things in the book that the boy pushes? What are some things that Newton pushes? What are some things that you might push?*

Something's location can be compared to other things around it (on, in, over, under, next to, etc.) Where are you right now? *Look at the pictures in the book and describe where the boy is, where the dog is, and where the toys are?*

Things can move in lines that can be straight, zigzag, or curved (such a circles). *Can you push (roll) a ball in each of these motions?*

You can describe how something moves (motion) by comparing it to other things around it. *Push (roll) a ball and describe how it moves by using "location" words. For example: The toy truck rolled down the sidewalk and stopped in a bush.*

Things can move at different speeds (fast. or slow). *Can you push (roll) a ball so it goes fast and slow? What are you doing to change the speed of the ball?*

How fast or slow something moves depends on how hard or soft the push or pull and how heavy the thing is. *Push (roll) balls of different sizes and weights (a ping pong ball, a tennis ball, a baseball, a basketball, or a bowling ball). If you push the ball with the same force, which one do you think will go farthest and why?*

Forces can change the direction of something that is moving. *Have someone push a ball toward you. What will you do to make the ball go the other way? What kind of force are you using? Can the other person use that same force to send the ball back to you again?*

Friction slows or stops something from moving (motion). *What are some of the friction forces that slow or stop things from moving in the book? What are some ways that you can slow or stop a ball from rolling? Does the surface the ball rolls on matter on how fast or far the ball rolls? Try rolling a ball on different surfaces to see.*

Gravity is a force that pulls things towards the Earth—what goes up will come down. *Can you throw anything in the air without it coming back down?*

Food for thought: What are some things you can do to help a ball roll fast and far? What do you think might happen if you push a ball twice as hard as a previous push?

Matching Forces

Decide which of the illustrations show pushes or pulls. Illustrations may apply to more than one force. Possible answers are upside down at the bottom of the page.

- When riding a bike, you push down on the pedals.
- A ball is pushed up into the air, but gravity pulls it back down again.
- The dad is pushing and the boy is pulling the wagon.
- Newton pushed one domino and each domino pushes another.

Who was Newton?

In this story, Newton is a dog. But in history, Sir Isaac Newton was a famous scientist and mathematician. Some of his many discoveries and contributions include:

- the law of gravity
- the laws of motion
- calculus
- the nature of light and color
- the cause of the tides (gravitational pull of the sun and the moon on the Earth)

Can you find any references to these statements in the illustrations?

- Newton was born in 1643 in Lincolnshire, England.
- It is said that he "discovered" gravity as he watched an apple fall from a tree.

Newton's Laws of Motion

The first two laws have been phrased for age appropriateness. Newton's third law is above the scope of this book and is not included.

1
Something won't move unless a force makes it move.

Once it starts moving, it will keep moving in a straight line until another force makes it move in another direction, slows it down, or stops it.

2
If you push something twice as hard, it will move twice as fast.

But if one thing is twice as heavy as another, it will only go half way.

To my parents, husband, and children who have always been supportive of my aspirations—LM

To the wonderful dogs in my life: Luke, Billy, Bailey, Buddy and Charlie, my faithful and always-happy friends—SR

Thanks to Susan Holmes, Senior Museum Educator at the Franklin Institute; Dr. Sigmund Abeles, (CT); and Marilyn Cook, teache and editor of Texas Council of Elementary Science's newsletter, for verifying the accuracy of the information in this book.

Publisher's Cataloging-In-Publication Data
Mayer, Lynne.   Newton and me / by Lynne Mayer ; illustrated by Sherry Rogers.

   p. : col. ill. ; cm.

  Summary: While at play with his dog, Newton, a young boy discovers the laws of force and motion in everyday activities such as throwing a ball, pulling a wagon, and riding a bike. Includes "For Creative Minds" section.

   Interest level: 4-8
   Grade level: P-3
   Lexile Level: 600, Lexile Code: AD
   ISBN: 978-1-60718-870-4 English hardcover
   ISBN: 978-1-60718-866-7 English paperback
   ISBN: 978-1-62855-397-0 Spanish paperback
   ISBN: 978-1 60718-092-0 English eBook downloadable
   ISBN: 978-1 60718-103-3 Spanish eBook downloadable
   ISBN: 978-1 60718-291-7 Interactive, read-aloud eBook featuring selectable English and Spanish text and audio (web and iPad/tablet based)

1. Force and energy--Juvenile literature. 2. Motion--Juvenile literature. 3. Physics--Juvenile literature. 4. Force and energy. 5. Motion. 6. Physics. I. Rogers, Sherry. II. Title.
QC25 .M394 2010
530   2009937784

Manufactured in the USA
This product conforms to CPSIA 2008
Sixth Printing

Arbordale Publishing
formerly Sylvan Dell Publishing
Mt. Pleasant, SC
www.ArbordalePublishing.com